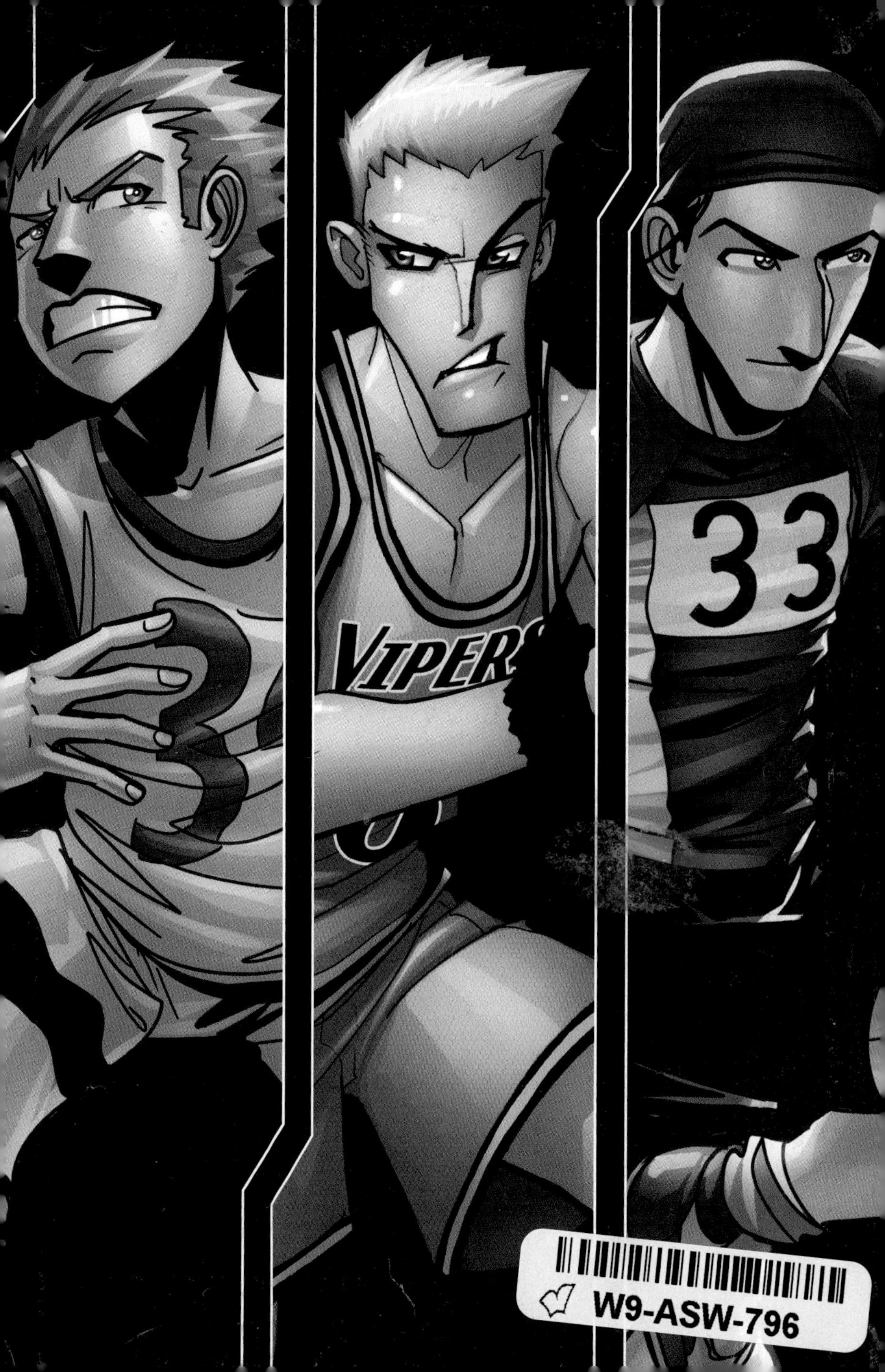
VIPERS
33

UP NEXT)))

:02   SPORTS ZONE SPECIAL REPORT

:04   FEATURE PRESENTATION:

QUARTERBACK SCRAMBLE

FOLLOWED BY:

:50   SPORTS ZONE POSTGAME RECAP

:51   SPORTS ZONE POSTGAME EXTRA

:52   SI KIDS INFO CENTER

STAR QUARTERBACK WES BLAKE SET TO BREAK STATE RECORD **SIK** *TICKER*

SPORTS ZONE
SPECIAL REPORT

FBL
FOOTBALL

PNT
PAINTBALL

SOC
SOCCER

BSL
BASEBALL

BBL
BASKETBALL

HKY

TWO HAWKS QUARTERBACKS DON'T SEE EYE-TO-EYE AT ALL

BEN PAULSON

STATS:
AGE: 14
POSITION: BACKUP QB

BIO: Ben Paulson doesn't mind being a benchwarmer. In fact, the very thought of stepping on the field to play quarterback makes him more than a little nervous. He's nothing like Wes Blake, who prefers to have the pressure placed squarely on his shoulders. However, rumors of Wes failing math class are making Ben more than a little worried about having to take over at quarterback.

UP NEXT: QUARTERBACK SCRAMBLE

WES BLAKE

AGE: 14

POSITION: STARTING QB

BIO: Wes is the perfect team captain. He's confident, quick, strong, and a born leader. His math skills, on the other hand, need a lot of work. Algebra may not be very useful on the field, but in order to stay in the game, Wes will have to pass math class.

Burlington Public Library
820 E Washington Ave
Burlington, WA 98233

BLZ vs BKS	3-1
TGR vs ROR	33-32
EAG vs BAN	14-7
SPA vs WLD	4-3
BAN vs ROR	21-15
RZR vs LIG	4-3
BLZ vs BKS	3-1

SHELDON COOPER

AGE: 14

BIO: Sheldon is excitable, friendly, and outgoing. He is the color commentator for the Eagles' football team.

MARIA ALVAREZ

AGE: 14

BIO: Maria is calm, cool, and collected. She is the play-by-play announcer for the Hawks.

MRS. SINGER

AGE: 34

BIO: Mrs. Singer teaches math. She's honest and fair, but expects a lot out of her students.

PRESENTS

QUARTERBACK SCRAMBLE

A PRODUCTION OF

STONE ARCH BOOKS
a capstone imprint

written by Brandon Terrell
illustrated by Gerardo Sandoval
colored by Benny Fuentes

designed and directed by Bob Lentz
edited by Sean Tulien
creative direction by Heather Kindseth
editorial management by Donald Lemke
editorial direction by Michael Dahl

Sports Illustrated KIDS *Quarterback Scramble* is published by Stone Arch Books,
151 Good Counsel Drive, P.O. Box 669, Mankato, Minnesota 56002.
www.capstonepub.com

Printed in the United States of America in Stevens Point, Wisconsin.
032013   007284R

Summary: Ben is happy to ride the bench — until the Hawks' star QB, Wes,
gets suspended for pulling poor grades in math. With Ben at the helm, the
offense stalls, and his teammates place the blame on his shoulders. Soon
after, a possible solution to his passing problems reveals itself — but
he's not so sure it's the right answer.

Library of Congress Cataloging-in-Publication Data
Terrell, Brandon, 1978-
   Quarterback scramble / written by Brandon Terrell ; illustrated by
Gerardo Sandoval and Benny Fuentes.
   p. cm. -- (Sports Illustrated kids graphic novels)
   ISBN 978-1-4342-2220-6 (library binding) -- ISBN 978-1-4342-3070-6 (pbk.)
1. Graphic novels. [1. Graphic novels. 2. Football--Fiction. 3. Self-
confidence--Fiction.] I. Sandoval, Gerardo, ill. II. Fuentes, Benny, ill. III.
Title.
PZ7.7.T46Qu 2011
741.5'973--dc22
                                               2010032920

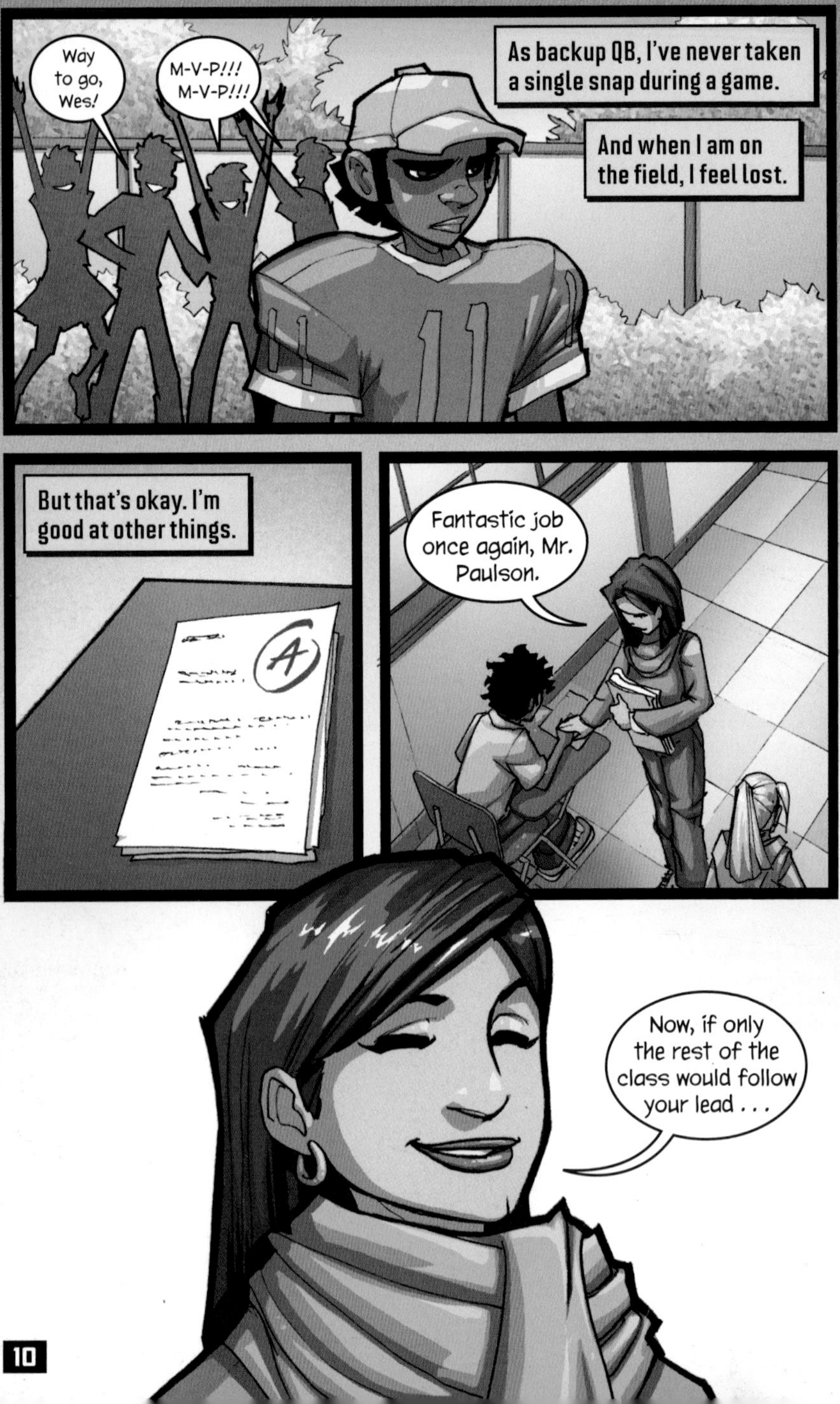

As backup QB, I've never taken a single snap during a game.
Way to go, Wes!
M-V-P!!! M-V-P!!!
And when I am on the field, I feel lost.
But that's okay. I'm good at other things.
Fantastic job once again, Mr. Paulson.
Now, if only the rest of the class would follow your lead . . .

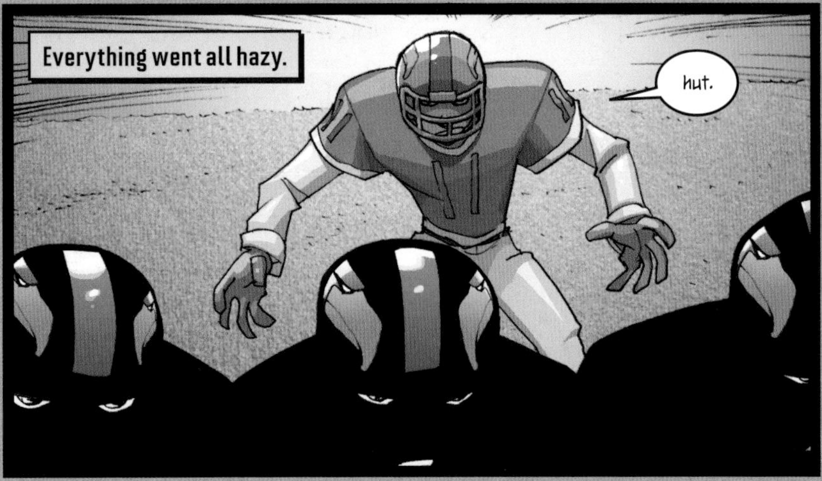
Everything went all hazy.
hut.

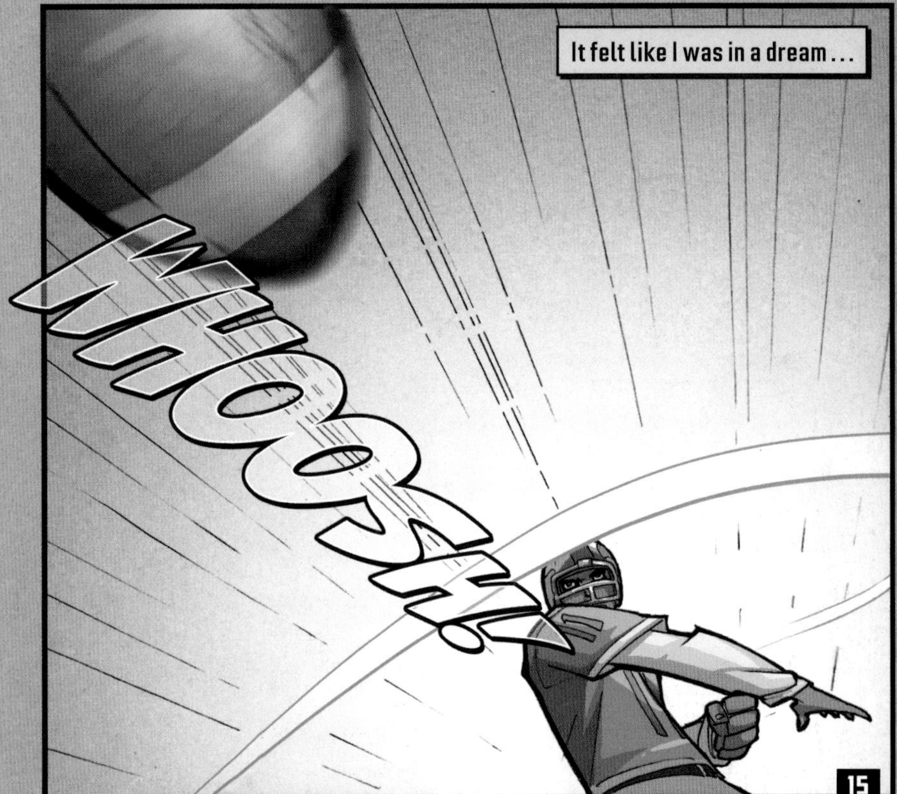
It felt like I was in a dream . . .
WHOOSH!

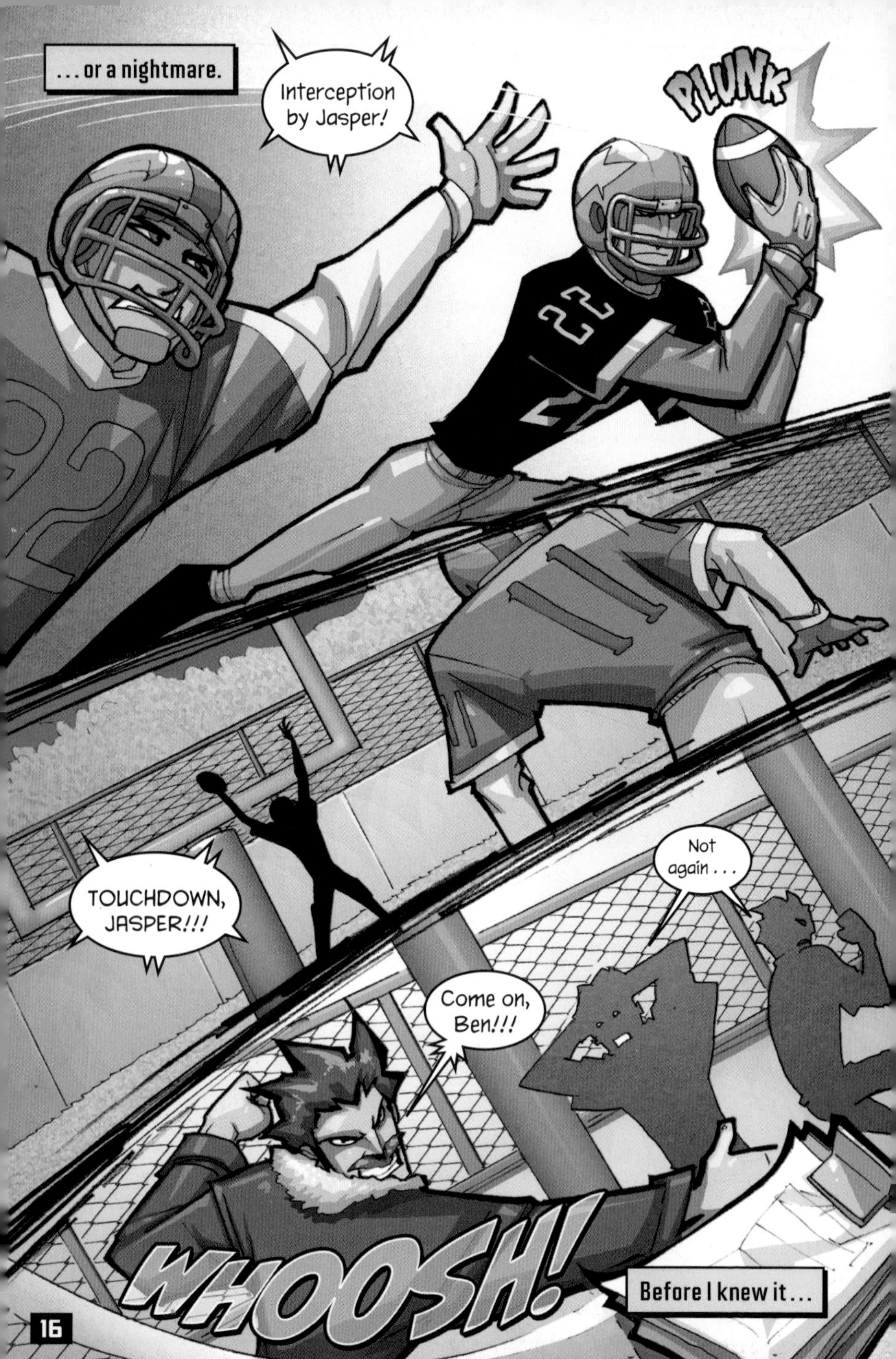
. . . or a nightmare.
Interception by Jasper!
PLUNK
TOUCHDOWN, JASPER!!!
Not again . . .
Come on, Ben!!!
WHOOSH!
Before I knew it . . .

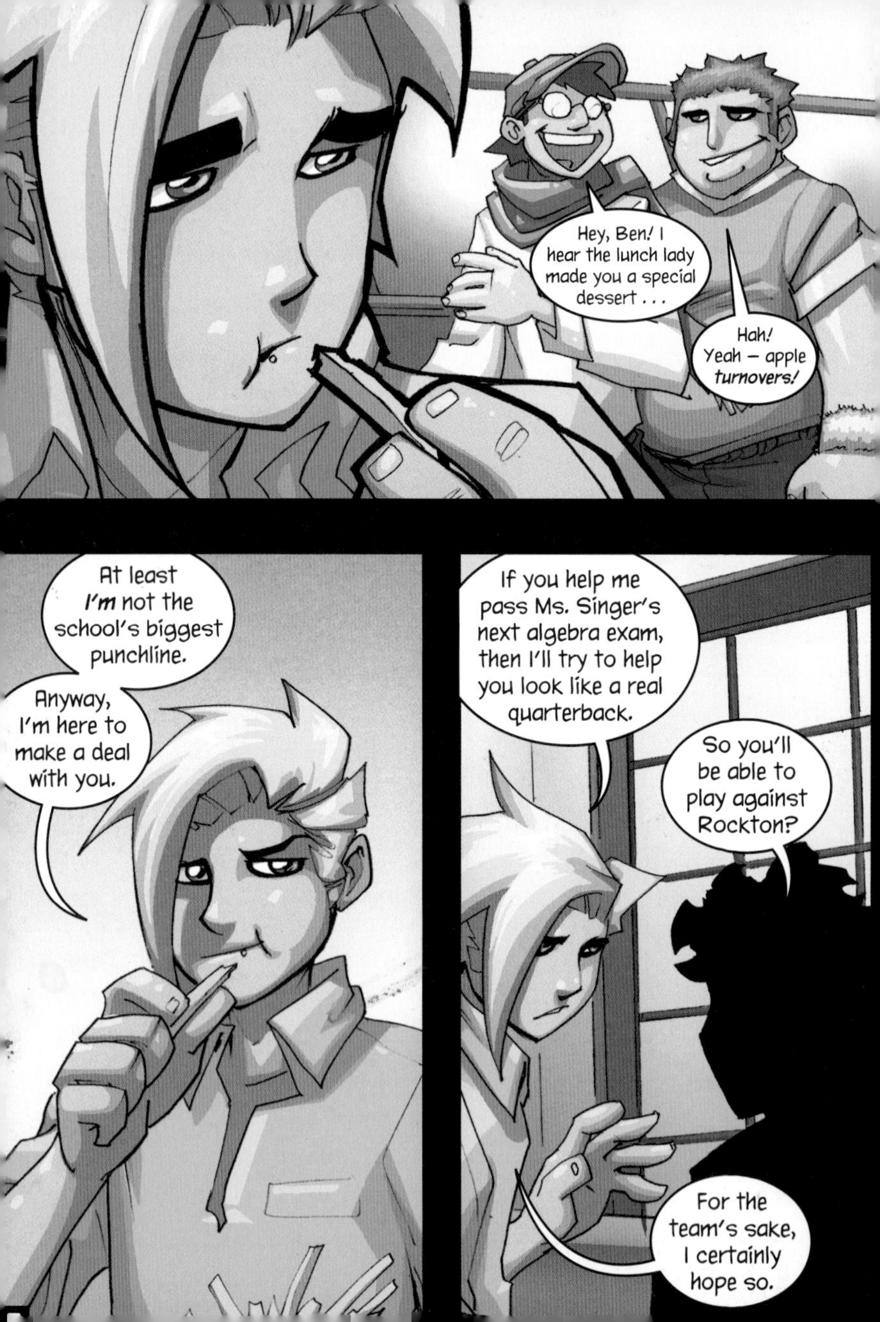
Hey, Ben! I hear the lunch lady made you a special dessert . . .
Hah! Yeah — apple *turnovers!*
At least *I'm* not the school's biggest punchline.
Anyway, I'm here to make a deal with you.
If you help me pass Ms. Singer's next algebra exam, then I'll try to help you look like a real quarterback.
So you'll be able to play against Rockton?
For the team's sake, I certainly hope so.

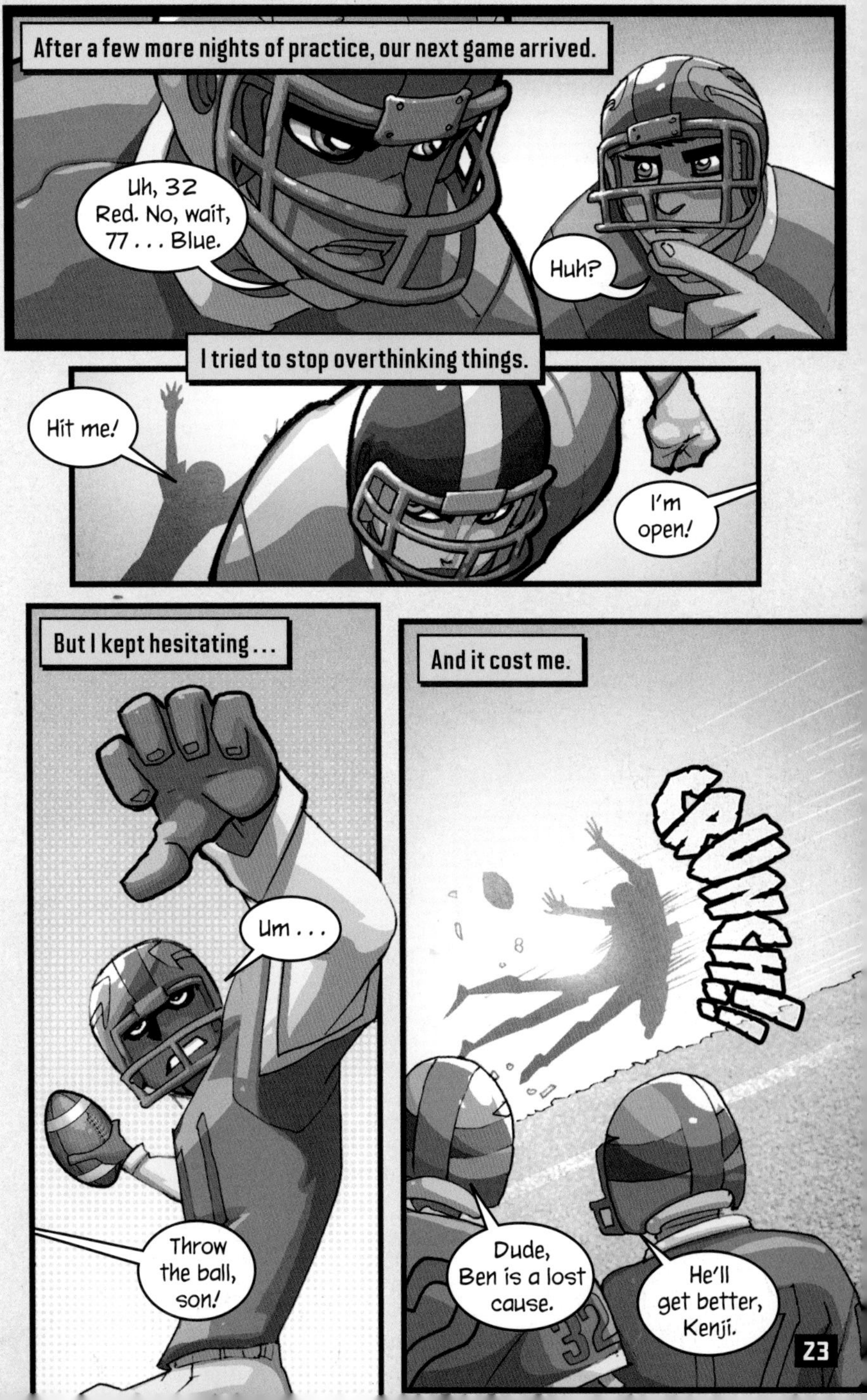

After a few more nights of practice, our next game arrived.
Uh, 32 Red. No, wait, 77 . . . Blue.
Huh?
I tried to stop overthinking things.
Hit me!
I'm open!
But I kept hesitating . . .
Um . . .
Throw the ball, son!
And it cost me.
CRUNCH!!
Dude, Ben is a lost cause.
He'll get better, Kenji.
32

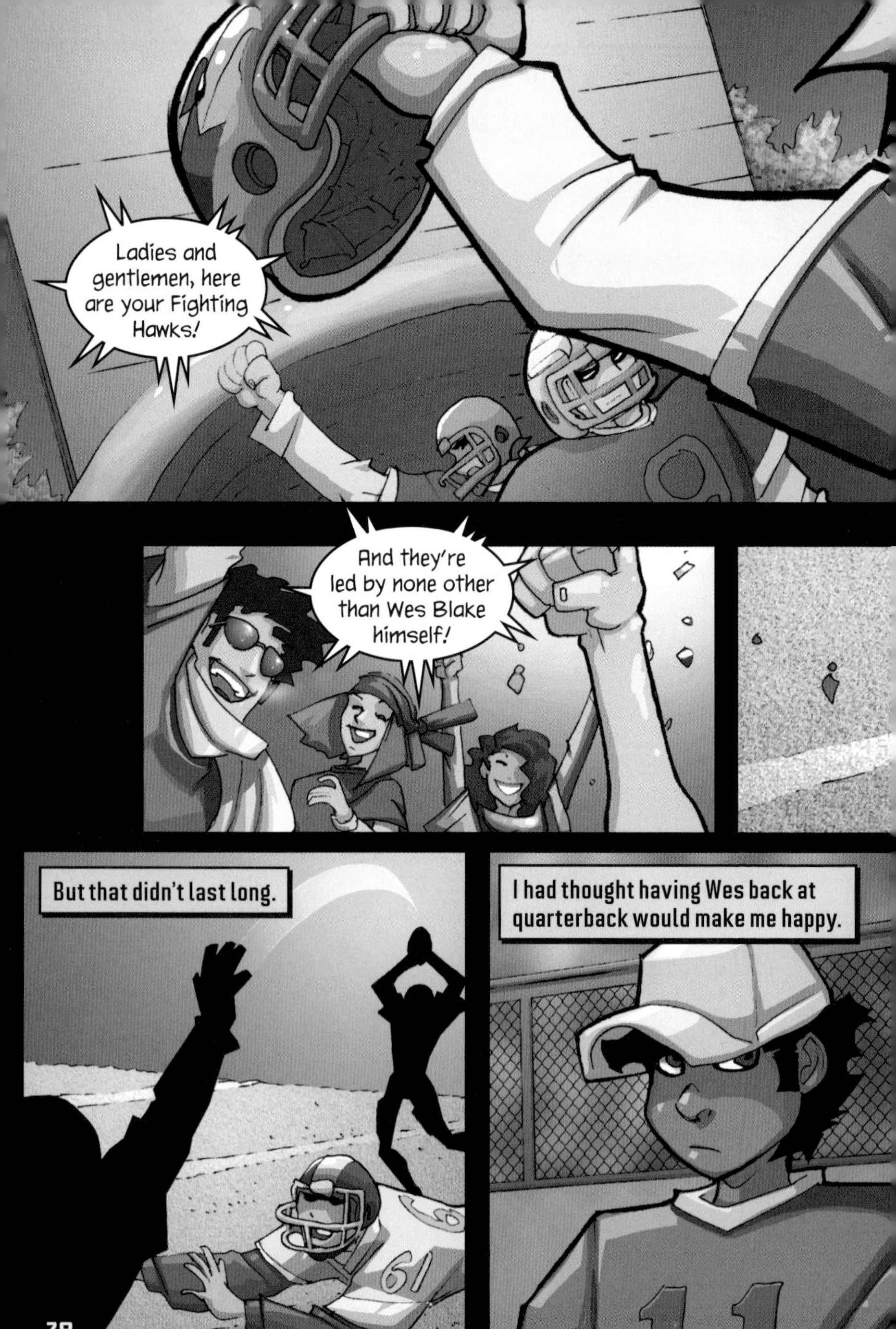
Ladies and gentlemen, here are your Fighting Hawks!
And they're led by none other than Wes Blake himself!
But that didn't last long.
61
I had thought having Wes back at quarterback would make me happy.

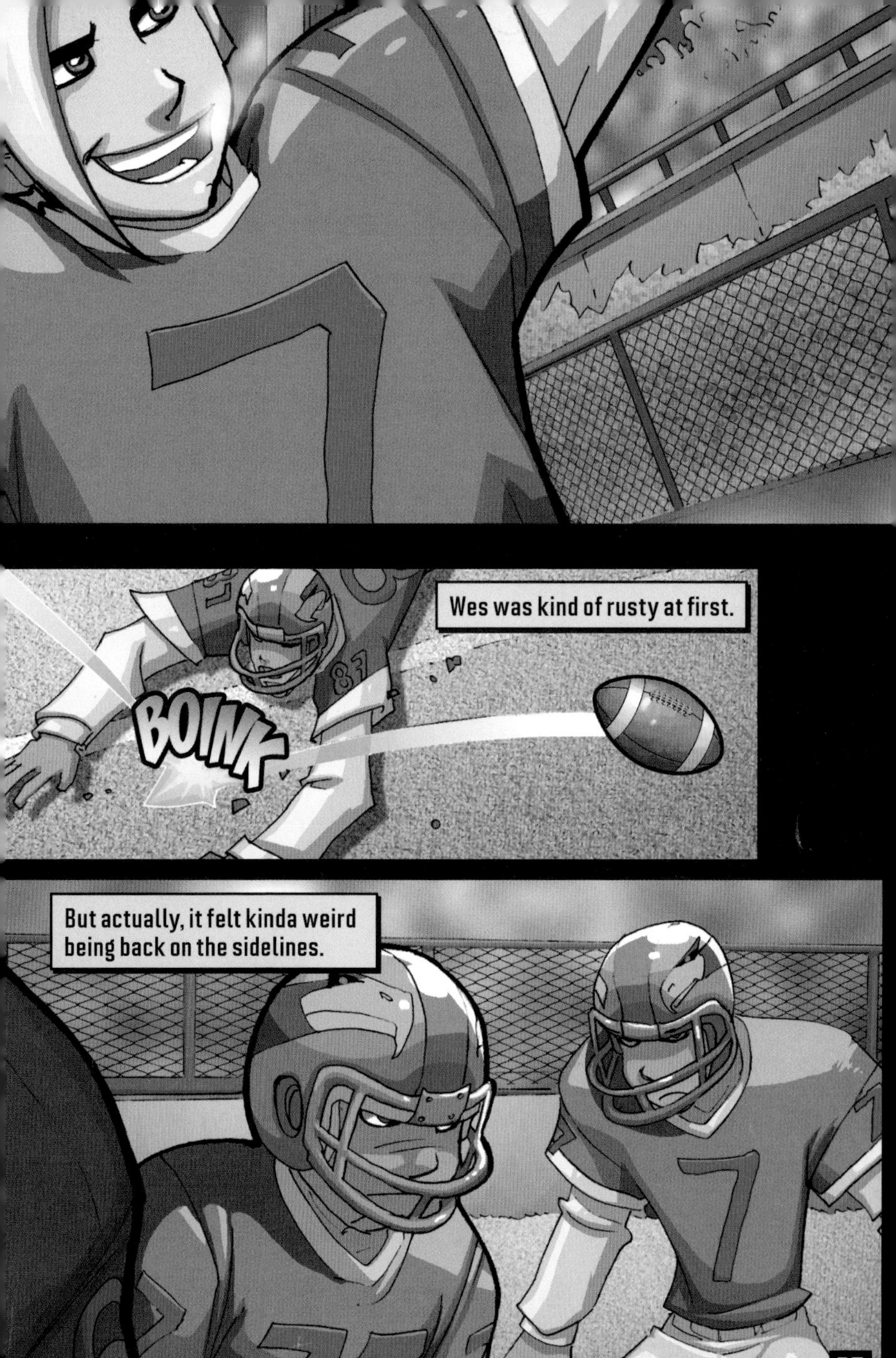
Wes was kind of rusty at first.
BOINK
But actually, it felt kinda weird being back on the sidelines.

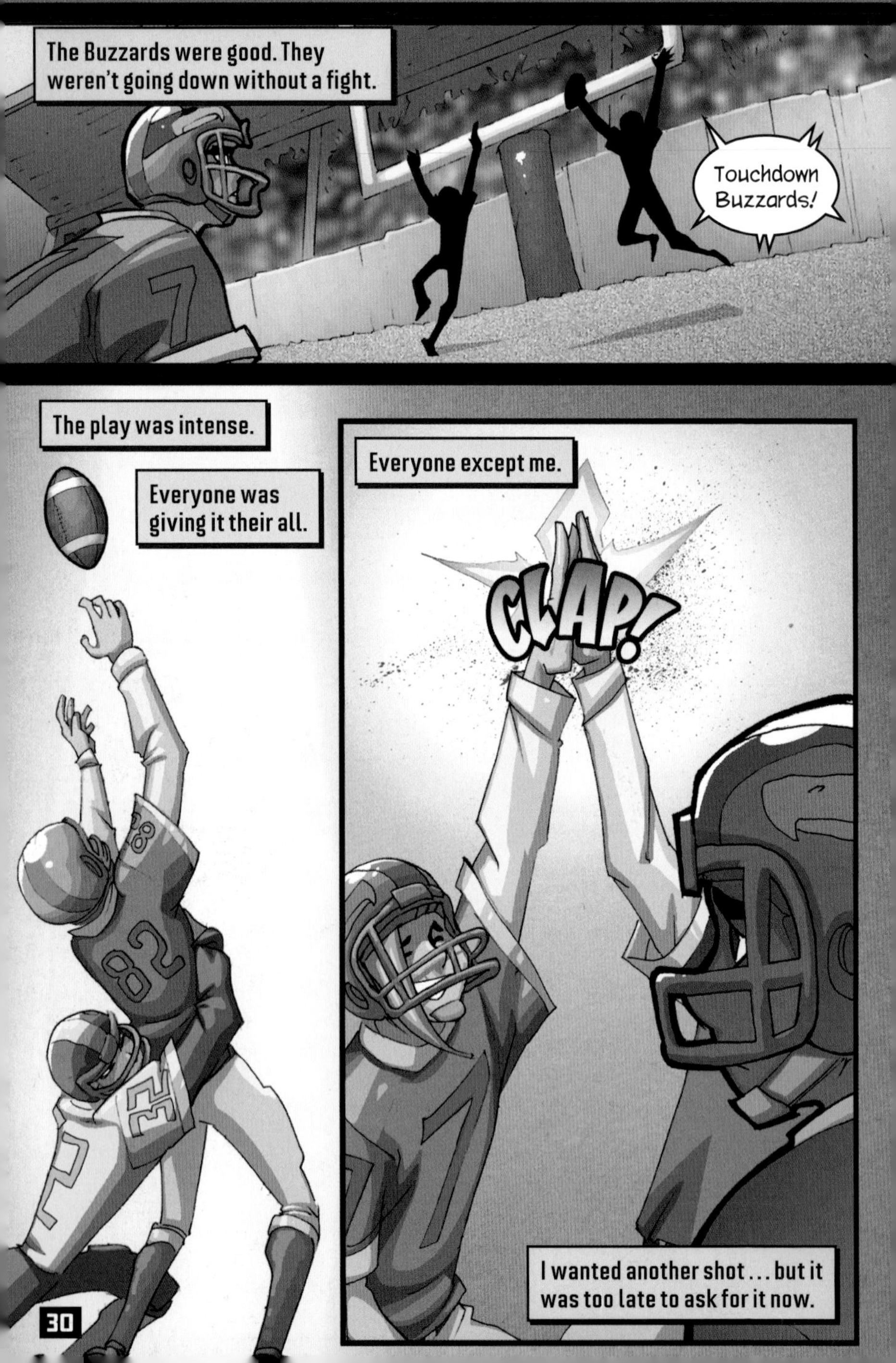
The Buzzards were good. They weren't going down without a fight.
Touchdown Buzzards!
The play was intense.
Everyone was giving it their all.
Everyone except me.
CLAP!
I wanted another shot . . . but it was too late to ask for it now.

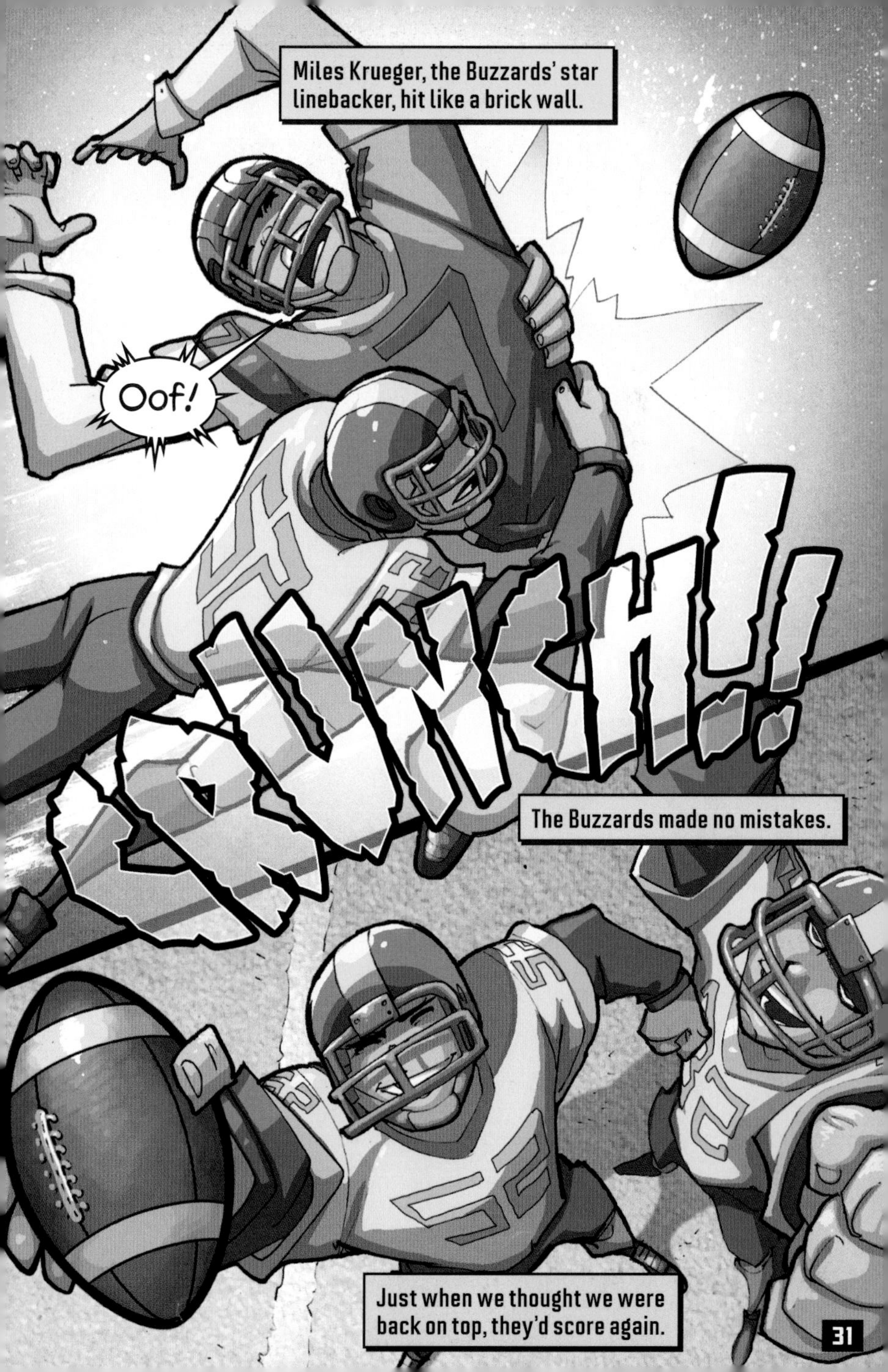
Miles Krueger, the Buzzards' star linebacker, hit like a brick wall.
Oof!
The Buzzards made no mistakes.
Just when we thought we were back on top, they'd score again.

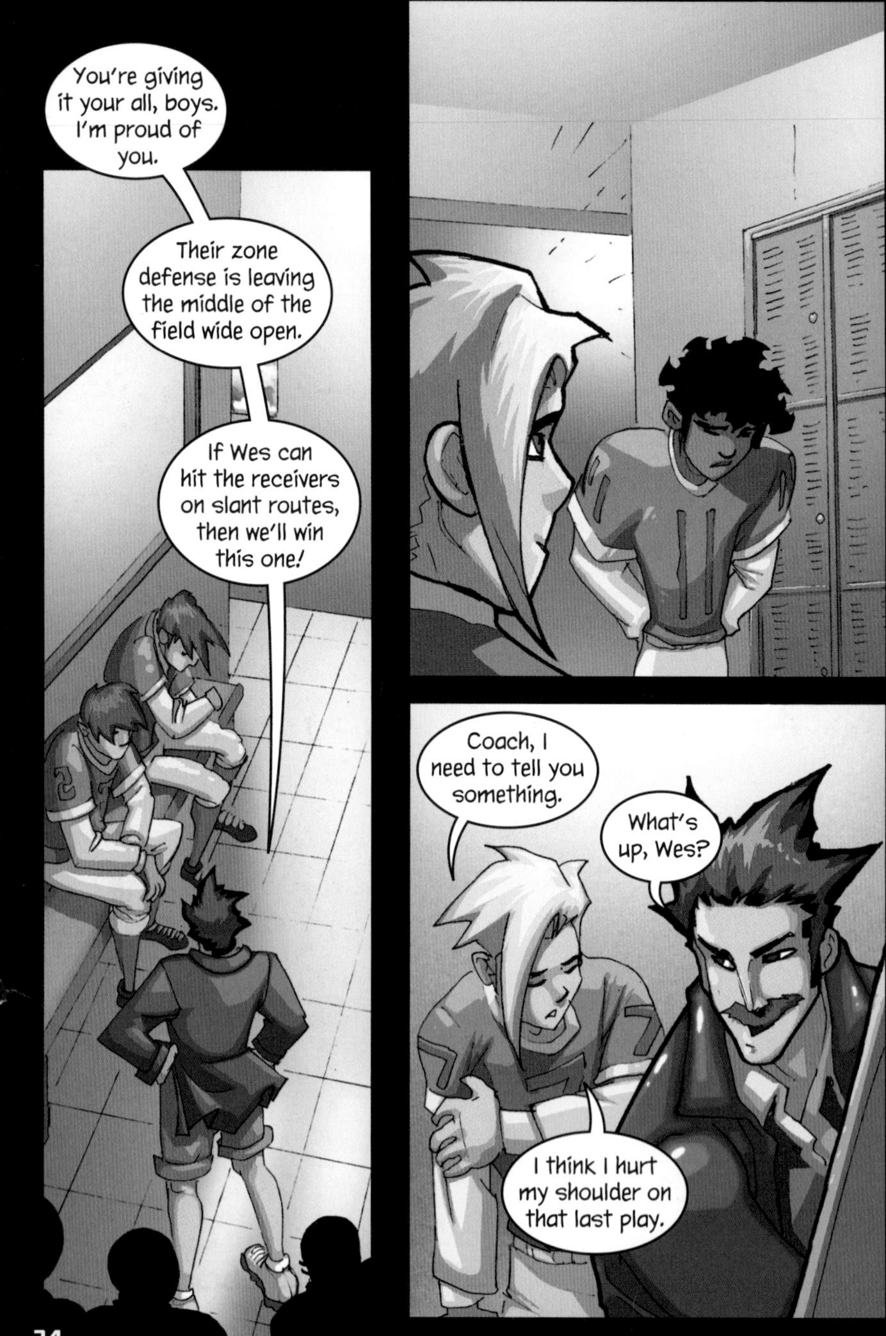

You're giving it your all, boys. I'm proud of you.
Their zone defense is leaving the middle of the field wide open.
If Wes can hit the receivers on slant routes, then we'll win this one!
Coach, I need to tell you something.
What's up, Wes?
I think I hurt my shoulder on that last play.

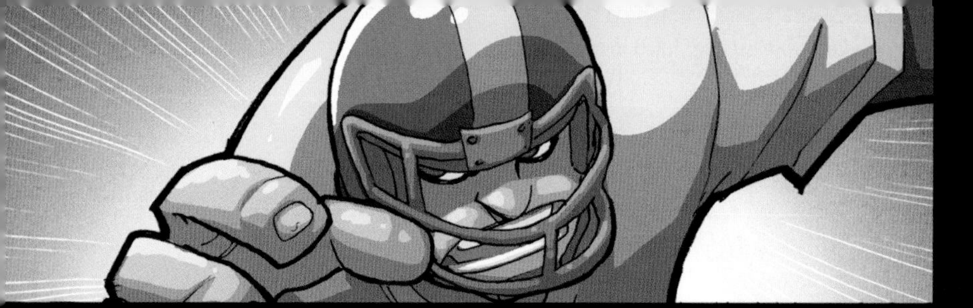

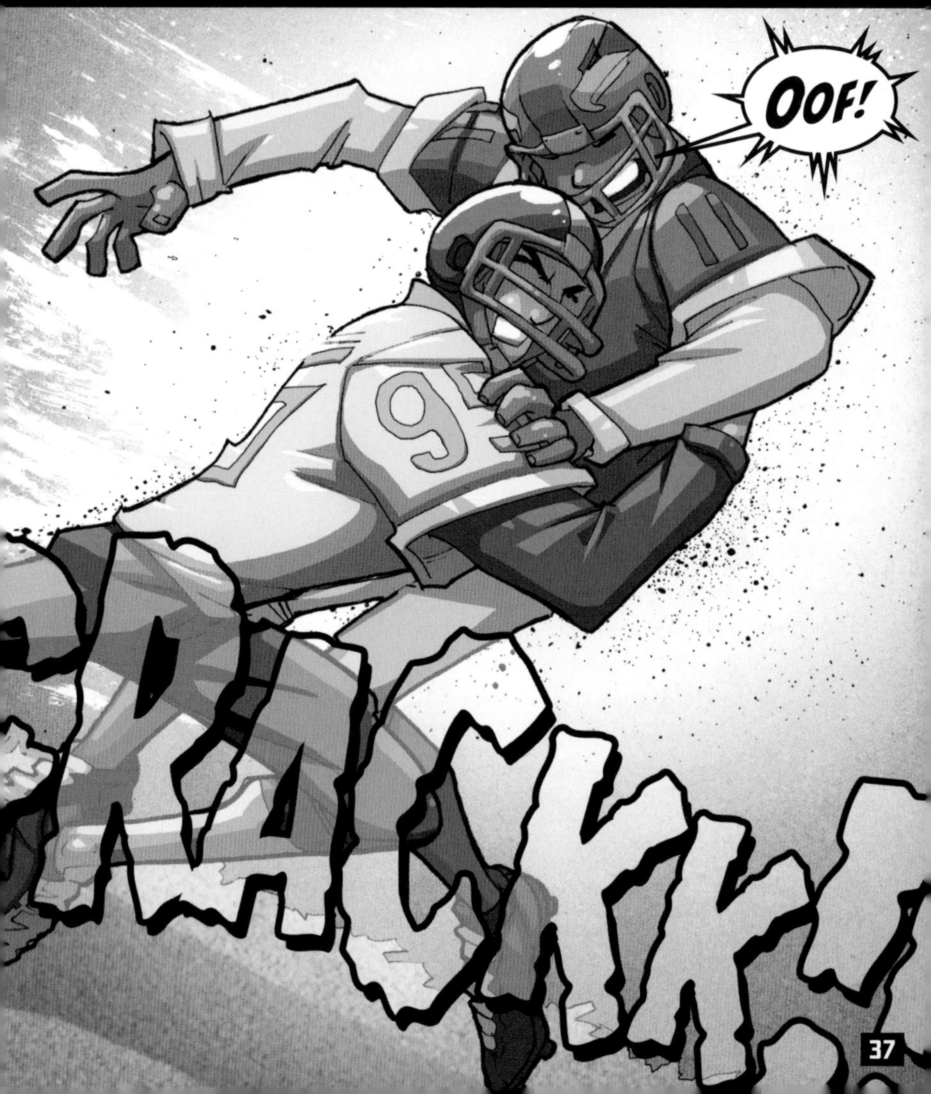
OOF!

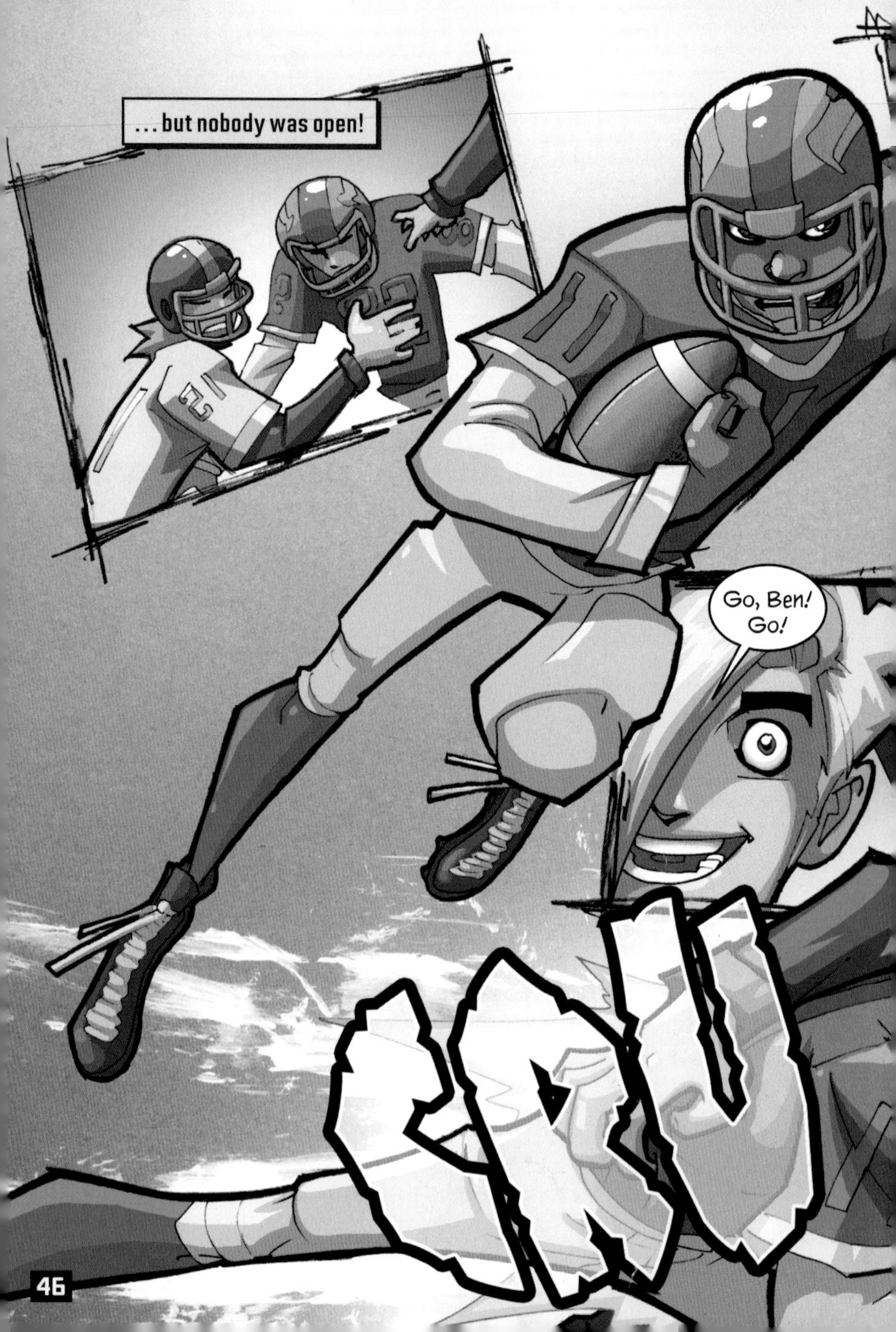

. . . but nobody was open!
Go, Ben! Go!

SPORTS ZONE

POSTGAME RECAP

FBL
FOOTBALL

PNT
PAINTBALL

SOC
SOCCER

BSL
BASEBALL

BBL
BASKETBALL

HKY

BEN PAULSON SURPRISES EVERYONE IN HAWKS' BIG WIN!

BY THE NUMBERS

STATS LEADERS:
TDs: PAULSON, 3
SACKS: KRUEGER, 4

STORY: Everyone was panicking when Wes Blake went down with an injured shoulder in the big game against the Buzzards. But when Ben Paulson stepped up, he shocked everyone by throwing multiple touchdowns and leading the Hawks to a come-from-behind victory. When asked how it felt, Ben said, "It was great to lead the team to a win — but I couldn't have done it without Wes Blake's help."

UP NEXT: SI KIDS INFO CENTER

SZ POSTGAME *EXTRA*

WHERE *YOU* ANALYZE THE GAME!

BLZ vs BHS
3-1
TGR vs RDR
33-32
EAG vs BAN
14-7
SPA vs WLD
4-3
BAN vs RDR
21-15
RDR vs LIG
4-3
BLZ vs BHS
3-1

Football fans got a real treat today when the Hawks faced off against the Buzzards in a memorable gridiron battle. Let's go into the stands and ask some fans for their opinions on the day's big game...

DISCUSSION QUESTION 1

Which quarterback do you like more — Ben Paulson or Wes Blake? Why?

DISCUSSION QUESTION 2

Do you play football? What's your favorite position? Which position is the hardest to play? Talk about football.

WRITING PROMPT 1

Wes and Ben helped each other out. Who have you helped? Who has helped you? What happened? Write about your helpful experiences.

WRITING PROMPT 2

Ben thinks confidence is important. What kinds of things are you confident about? What aren't you confident about? Write about it!

INFO CENTER

GLOSSARY

BLITZ (BLITS)—a play where the defense tries to tackle the quarterback right after the snap

CERTIFIED (SUR-tuh-fied)—guaranteed to be genuine or real

CONFIDENT (KON-fuh-duhnt)—having a strong belief in yourself

EPIC (EP-ik)—heroic or impressive

HAZY (HAYZ-ee)—unclear or out of focus

HESITATING (HEZ-uh-tate-ing)—pausing before doing something due to uncertainty

INTENSE (in-TENSS)—very strong or overwhelming

PRESSURE (PRESH-ur)—strong influence or strain

PUNCH LINE (PUHNCH LINE)—the part of the joke that makes people laugh

SLANT ROUTE (SLANT ROUT)—a pattern run by a receiver where the receiver runs up the field at about a 45-degree angle

CREATORS

Brandon Terrell › Author
Brandon Terrell is a writer and filmmaker who has worked in the Minnesota film and television community for nearly ten years. He is the author of the graphic novel *Horrorwood*, published by Ape Entertainment. He is also an avid baseball fan, and is crazy about the Minnesota Twins. Terrell lives in Saint Paul with his wife, Jennifer.

Gerardo Sandoval › Illustrator
Gerardo Sandoval is a professional comic book illustrator from Mexico. He has worked on many well-known comics including Tomb Raider books from Top Cow Production. He has also worked on designs for posters and card sets.

Benny Fuentes › Colorist
Benny Fuentes lives in Villahermosa, Tabasco in Mexico, where the temperature is just as hot as the sauce. He studied graphic design in college, but now he works as a full-time colorist in the comic book and graphic novel industry for companies like Marvel, DC Comics, and Top Cow Productions. He shares his home with two crazy cats, Chelo and Kitty, who act like they own the place.

Sports Illustrated KIDS GRAPHIC NOVELS
QUICK COMIC

TOU YANG IN:
KICKOFF BLITZ

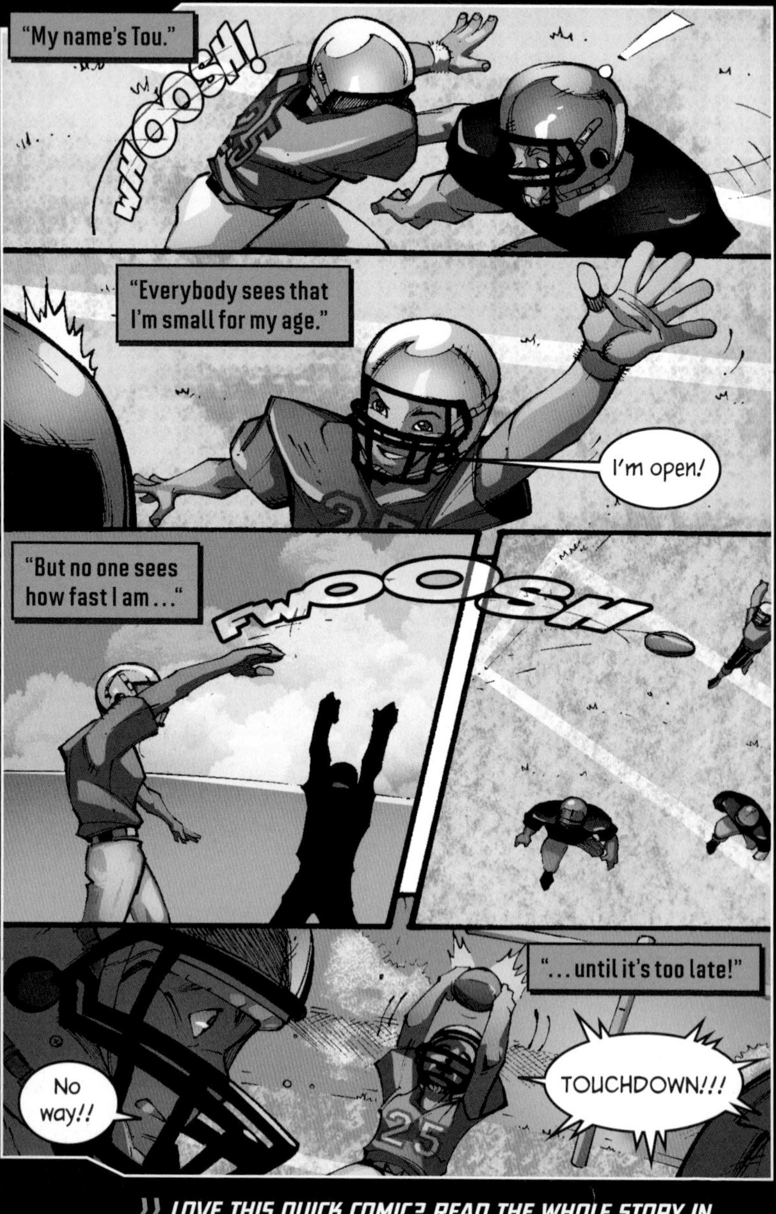
"My name's Tou."
WHOOOSH!
"Everybody sees that I'm small for my age."
I'm open!
"But no one sees how fast I am . . ."
FWOOOSH
". . . until it's too late!"
No way!!
TOUCHDOWN!!!

» LOVE THIS QUICK COMIC? READ THE WHOLE STORY IN KICKOFF BLITZ – ONLY FROM STONE ARCH BOOKS!

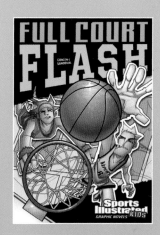

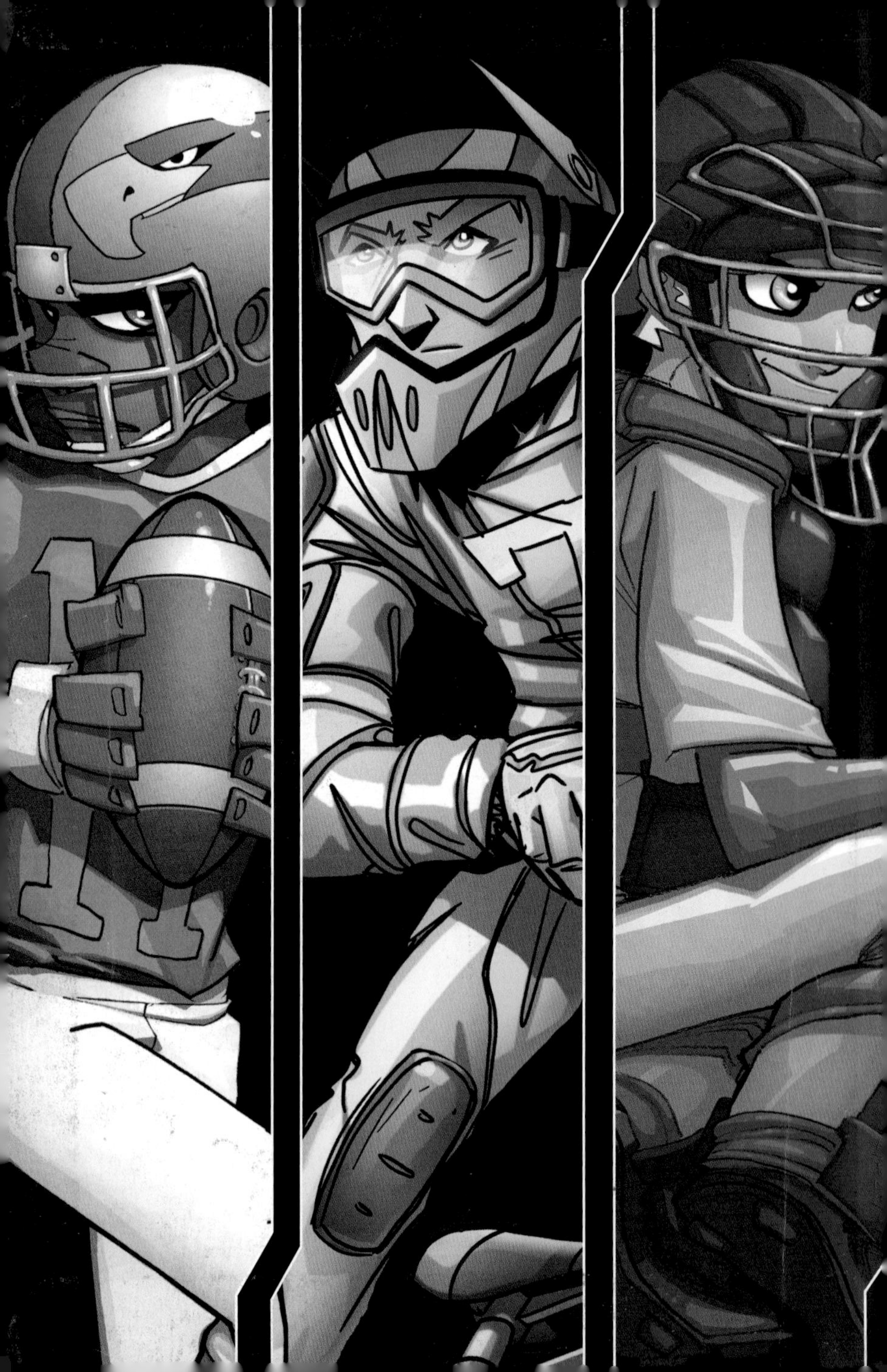